KU-784-638

START Talking

When I'm a Grown-up

Copyright © QED Publishing 2004

First published in the UK in 2004 by
QED Publishing
A division of Quarto Publishing plc
The Fitzpatrick Building
188–194 York Way, London N7 9QP

All rights reserved. No part of this publication may be reproduced, stored in a
retrieval system, or transmitted in any form or by any means, electronic,
mechanical, photocopying, recording, or otherwise, without the prior permission
of the publisher, nor be otherwise circulated in any form of binding or cover
other than that in which it is published and without a similar condition being
imposed on the subsequent purchaser.

A Catalogue record for this book is
available from the British Library.

ISBN 1 84538 007 X

Written by Anne Faundez
Designed by Alix Wood
Editor Hannah Ray
Illustrated by Katherine Lucas

Series Consultant Anne Faundez
Creative Director Louise Morley
Editorial Manager Jean Coppendale

Printed and bound in China

ROTHERHAM LIBRARY & INFORMATION SERVICES	
B48 2210285	
Askews	
YC	£9.99
	RO 00005102 4

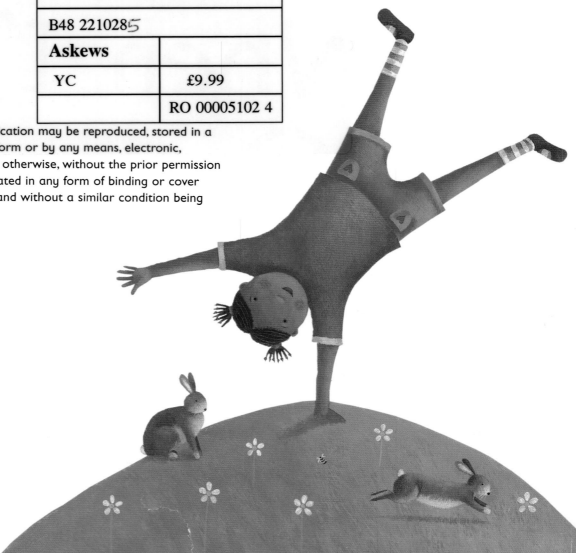

B48 221 028 5   SLS

SCHOOLS LIBRARY SERVICE
MALTBY LIBRARY HEADQUARTERS
HIGH STREET
MALTBY
ROTHERHAM   -- JAN 2005
S66 8LD

START
Talking

When I'm a Grown-up

Anne Faundez

QED Publishing

QED

When I'm a grown-up,
Who will I be?

A bird in the air,

Or a fish in the sea?

5

When I'm a grown-up,
What will I do?

6

Fly a spaceship to Mars,
Or work in a zoo?

7

When I'm a grown-up,
Will I be tall?

8

Huge like a hippo,

Or round like a ball?

9

When I'm a grown-up,
What will I eat?

10

Pineapple pie,
Or some other treat?

When I'm a grown-up,

Who will live with me?

A frog or a dog?

Or a hoppity flea?

15

When I'm a grown-up,
What will I wear?

Hmm, let me see,
I really don't care!

When I'm a grown-up,
Will I travel by car?

Ride on a rhino,

Or swing from a star?

19

When I'm a grown-up,
I really don't mind
Who I will be –

As long as
I'm
ME!

21

What do you think?

Can you spot the fairy cakes? What other types of food can you see?

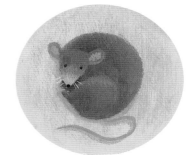

Can you remember any of the animals that appear in the story?

What does the little girl think she might do when she is a grown-up?

Who might live with the little girl when she is a grown-up?

Carers' and teachers' notes

- Together, look at the front cover. Read the title to your child.
- Read the story aloud, pointing to the words as you do so.
- Talk about the illustrations on pages 6–7. How many elephants can your child see? Can your child spot the owl?
- Look closely at the illustrations throughout the book and talk about what's happening in each one. Which sections of the pictures show the reality of the little girl's life, and which show her fantasies of being a grown-up?
- Act out pages 4–5 by encouraging your child to ask the question 'When I'm a grown-up, who will I be?' and then miming the actions of a bird flying in the air and a fish swimming in the sea.
- Ask your child what he/she would like to be when he/she's a grown-up.

- Ask your child what food he/she would choose to eat when he/she's a grown-up.
- Which is your child's favourite picture? Why does he/she like that particular picture the most?
- Encourage your child to draw two pictures: one, a portrait of himself/herself and the other, a picture of what your child would like to be when he/she's a grown-up.
- Talk about rhyming words, for example 'tall' and 'ball', 'me' and 'flea'. What other rhyming words are there in this story?
- Together, think of some more words which rhyme with those in the story, for example 'pie' – try, lie.
- Encourage your child to tell you the story in his/her own words, using the illustrations as prompts. Your child does not have to stick rigidly to the original text but can interpret the illustrations in his/her own way.